Dixie Mountain Mystery

Mystery

LOLA SMITH

Order this book online at www.trafford.com
or email orders@trafford.com

Most Trafford titles are also available at major online book retailers.

Printed in the United States of America.

ISBN: 978-1-4907-5377-5 (sc)
ISBN: 978-1-4907-5376-8 (e)

Trafford rev. 01/13/2015

 www.trafford.com

North America & international
toll-free: 1 888 232 4444 (USA & Canada)
fax: 812 355 4082

Acknowledgements

THANK YOU TO MY WONDERFUL husband Dennis, we had 62 years of marriage and six great children together. Without him, there wouldn't have been any story to tell. **I would like this book to be a tribute to my husband Dennis H. Smith Sr.**

This story would not have been written if it wasn't for my daughter, Jolynn Rose. By pushing me into the electronic age. Because without the electronic age, I would not of took on this challenge. We are also working on our fourth book together.

Thanks to Gary Rose for helping put this book together, and the rest of my wonderful family for their support.

This book will live long after I am gone!

God bless everyone!

Prologue

THIS STORY IS BASED ON some true facts about us living on Dixie Mountain in 1958. I am now 81 years old; it hasn't been easy for me to write this book. I started this story when I was in my twenties. I never dreamed I would ever finish this book and get it published.

It is about one very long summer on Dixie Mountain. My husband Dennis and I thought we would take our very young children out to live in the country. We found ourselves roughing it on sixteen undeveloped acres. Little did we know, what was in store for us on Dixie Mountain and the mystery we would find.

I wrote this book partly for our children. I hope they enjoy it and everyone else too.

The adventure and the mystery of Dixie Mountain!

Chapter 1

REGARDLESS OF THE MODERN PROGRESS and the fast-moving pace of today there still seems to be that small spark of the old pioneering spirit in a good many of us.

Just about every weekend, my husband and I would pile our six children in the car and drive out in the country, the kids loved it! They still remember the bologna sandwiches and pop that we would get from a country store. Also the songs we would attempt to sing. They had no idea we were looking at property that might be for sale. We felt the country would be a good place to raise our children. We were both young and healthy enough to take on the "challenge."

We decide to get serious; we got a sitter for the kids and called a real estate man, to look at some farms. We had found nothing to interest us till we turned off onto a gravel road. It was very narrow, but thought we would see where it went. There was a shack on the right side of the road but we kept going. The road seems to be going along the hilltop. As we drove on there was a little green house to our right. A little farther on there was an open field down below us, we continued on. Then there were more woods and finally it came to an end and there was another open field and there stood a tall barn. Although, it had turned gray from the weather, it stood brave and almost defiant against all odds. We sat in silence just looking. For myself I have the feeling this was it, if it was for sale.

We drove back to the little green house, which we had passed earlier, to see if they knew anything about the property. The sixty some year old real estate man, that walked a little bent over and had a rather weathered looking face with tired looking eyes. He got out of the car and went to the door and knocked.

The wind had come up and was whipping his suit jacket about him. As he waited at the door for someone to answer, we saw him enter. But did not see who had let him in. About a half hour later he came out again. A tall thin man with reddish hair and beard followed him out to the car. We got out of the car to greet him.

As it turned out he was the owner. The tall man seemed very pleased with the idea of selling the piece of land. He introduced himself as Ted Jones. Ted told us there was 16 acres with two thirds cleared and was completely fenced in. It had two fair size sheds and a log cabin that was over 100 years old.

We all walked down over the knoll and sure enough there was an old cabin nestled very close to the hillside. It was very impressive. There were wide windows the full length of the front side of the cabin. We had to go around to the right side of the cabin to get into the door.

It was starting to get dusk by now; it was dark inside of the cabin. The owner walked slowly into the center of the one large room, and found a long string hanging from a light and turned it on. I remember thinking thank goodness it has electricity! As light filled the one and only room we saw an old iron cook stove covered with dust and spider webs. Sitting by the door a small cupboard with three shelves stood in the far corner. An open stairway led to one large bedroom that had a small window to let in the light. The inside of the roof was covered with tarpaper, which was torn in places. There was so much dust, you could see everywhere we touched or walked. I was getting very doubtful now, especially when we found there was no plumbing, "of course." The back part of the cabin that was built back into the hill was not livable. So it was just the main part of the cabin to make it livable. Oh my!

About 20 yards from the cabin was an old-fashioned hand pump sitting on a wooden platform, next to it was a small delightful pond. The scotch bloom bushes had pretty well taken over all around the cabin, but all we could see was how it would look after we got it all cleaned out.

The dirt road we had seen before had come down from the barn and passed in front of the cabin. We walked up the road to take a look at the barn. It was much taller than I thought. There were some repairs to be made. Dennis was very impressed. I couldn't help feel the warmth and protection that the big old barn offered. It had been built completely by hand, from the uncut beams to the handmade shingles on the steep roof.

We then left the barn and crossed an open field back to the car. The only animal in the barn was a curious three-year-old black calf. As we walked across the field the calf followed us. The real estate man was trailing behind us gazing about as he walked. The calf was right behind him sniffing the legs of his trousers; all at once the calf licked his britches, at the same time the man gave a startled jump into the air, letting out a shrill oooooh! We couldn't help laughing. It looked as though the calf had lifted him up with his long tongue, the calf took off running. The real estate man mopped his brow with his handkerchief and quickly got in front of us, looking a little distressed and gave a little giggle of relief.

Chapter 2

THAT EVENING AT HOME, WE talked over the advantages of living in the country. My husband and I both had spent most of our childhood living on a farm, so it would not be entirely new to us. We decided to purchase the 16 acres, in spite of the inconveniences. The deal was made and at a very reasonable price.

I worried a little about our young children having so much space to run around in. We were fortunate to rent out our house in town, right away. My husband had a good job in town and said he didn't mind the 20 mile drive. He was working swing shift at the time. We figured we could make the cabin livable.

Later after everything was settled we started cleaning and getting the cabin ready to move into. At first I stood looking at all the cleaning to be done and felt it was hopeless. How on earth are we going to get all the beds in here? What about all the furniture? Oh dear! What have we gotten ourselves into? Dennis stepped in and said, "We can put this there and that there. He was bursting with enthusiasm. I could not help to join in. I put a scarf around my head and put on gloves. I cleaned and scrubbed till I was blue in the face. After scrubbings the old cook stove it was amazing what good shape it was in. Oh Yeah! It had a tank on the right side for heating water! Yea! It took the place as keeper of the cabin.

When we told the kids earlier about moving we got different reactions from them.

Jill our eight year old daughter was a little doubtful and asked "Where do we go to school? She had long brown hair with pretty blue eyes like her mom (me).

Sharlene our seven year old, who also had brown hair and blue eyes, which sometimes turned green said, "Oh good that might be fun."

Jolynn our six year old, who had light brown hair that would turn almost blond in the summer and pretty blue eyes, spoke up "I don't want to ride a dumb old bus!" I told her "You won't for awhile."

Our boy Chris is five years old, also has brown hair and blue eyes. He piped up and said "It's ok by me, do we get animals?"

Our four year old Dennis with very dark hair and very brown eyes like his dad said, "Yeah, I want a dog!"

Our youngest who is three year old Darren said, "Can I take my toys?" He too had dark hair and very brown eyes like his dad.

Ok, kids it's like this. I said you girls have all summer before you have to go to school. Yes, Chris I guess we will have animals. Probably a dog Denny, and Darren you get to bring your toys. Ok?

I know they were all close in age, but I never regretted it. I guess Dennis Sr. and I were petty fertile. No we are not Catholics. We realize that the best time in our lives was raising our children. I am five foot two inches and Dennis is five nine. We were a real nice fit. Oh Yeah!

Now the hard part! Moving something's into storage and the rest up to the cabin. We didn't have much room in the cabin, so a lot of our things had to go into storage. My brothers jumped in to help us move, it was a lot of work but my brother made it fun.

Chapter 3

I HAD NOT STOPPED TO think about the kids and I being alone at night. My husband had no choice but to work the swing shift, leaving us alone from 3:00 p.m. to 1:00 a.m. Being ignorantly brave I reassured him we would be alright.

As night came and the children were all tucked into bed, I slowly started losing my courage. I felt so alone. It was so opposite of town life, where there were street lights, and the usual city noises, to give you the reassuring feeling that people were close by. This was one of the things I found hardest to get used to.

Finding that there was no fresh water, I took the water bucket and headed out to the well, telling myself there wasn't anything to be afraid of. To my relief the night was warm and the stars were shining brightly. As I got to the pump, I realized the frogs in the upper pasture were starting to crock. As I began filling the pail, it seemed that other frogs started joining in. The sound became louder and the still night echoing it even louder. I pumped faster now and tried to whistle as I looked about me, half expecting to see the frogs, hopping down the field. Realizing suddenly that the pail was full and running over. I stopped my frantic pumping. I grabbed the pail and nearly drop it. I tried to run to the house; with a full bucket of water, that was spilling all over me as I ran. I cared about nothing but getting inside the cabin. Half running and half stumbling I went as if the devil was after me. Once inside I slammed the door shut. Leaning against the door and puffing I looked down at the pail, it had just about four inches of water in the bottom. With a sigh as I set down the pail. It wasn't till then I notice my pant legs of my jeans were dripping with water. I went upstairs to change, with my shoe squishing all the way. As the evening grew later and later even the radio and doing my chores about the cabin didn't help. I finally decided to retired. I put the 22 rifle under the bed, just in case some creature might get into the house.

Laying there wide-eyed, I stared into the darkness, with only a faint sound of my enemies croaking off into the distance. My eyes began to slowly close, but my ears were straining to hear any little sound that was familiar and reassuring, like the refrigerator turning on, or a passing car on the distant gravel road.

Chapter 4

Just as I started to doze the jingling of a belt buckle startled me, I jumped out of bed. After grabbing for the light string, I turned on the light. There between the beds on the floor was a large gray digger with the pant leg of one of the boy's jean's in his mouth, staring at me. The belt still in the pants made the jingling noise, as the animals scampered towards a hole, it had found under the eve of the roof.

Not even thinking of the rifle, I quickly crept after the thief, and grabbed a hold of the pants, as it tried to pull them through the hole. I held on determined not to let him have them. I gave a little tug, but not too hard for the fear that the gray digger would come out with the pants. It tug right back, I tugged again, it wouldn't let go, so I gave a good yank and landed on the floor as it let go and disappeared. I decided to wait up for my husband, I was so glad to see him. I don't think I have ever been happier to see anyone in my life, as I was when he arrived home.

A gray digger is a type of rodent that looks like an oversize squirrel, with gray fur and a rat-like tail. Most of the rodents such as pack rats, mice, and gray digger's were pretty determined not to be kicked out of their comfortable home. This gave me many a sleepless nights.

Just as determined as they, I set out poison and traps. I made sure all food was tightly covered and stored safely away. All garbage was quickly disposed of.

I finally won the battle with persistence. About a week later a neighbor woman, while visiting me, asked if we had been getting rid of the rats. I replied I had and was taking measures to see they didn't return. She said "I thought so! I think they moved over to our house."

Chapter 5

WHEN DENNIS GOT HOME THAT first evening, we sat down with a cup of coffee before going to bed. Dennis said "Guess what? I am going on dayshift starting Monday." I could tell he was sure glad for the change. He said, he was worried about me and the kids here alone at night we were both happy about the change. I decided not to tell him about my evening.

The next couple weeks Dennis would come home with something: first it was four Angus's calves, then 12 almost grown chickens, also shingles for the roof.

The neighbors asked if they could pasture their milk cow and we would get half share of milk. We agreed. She turned out to be a very affectionate cow. She thought she was part of the family, and every time I happen to leave the cabin door open, she went into the cabin and made herself right at home. I would have to get the kids to help me get her out, because she was so stubborn.

The chickens thought they had their rights too, until we got them fenced in. The dog (that daddy brought home) was a little mutt, so that's what we called him. Now the dog wasn't going to be left out of things and continually tried to sneak into the house. Each time he did there was a big commotion to get him out again. There just wasn't room for him. Mutt also thought that the chickens were his pets, every morning at sunrise; he would greet them with a bark and herd them back into the coop. Then they would try to escape again, and Mutt was there to herd them back in again. This would go on until, I yelled at him to stop it.

One day I had baked a birthday cake for Jolynn, I put it in the open window to cool. Well Mutt got in again and of course there was a commotion, with all of us chasing him about; to catch him, and put him outside of the cabin. The excited dog gave a leap out the window and in the process put one foot into the side of the cake!

Throwing my hands up in despair, I sat down and tried very hard to keep my temper under control. Seeing the cake had not been entirely destroyed, I cut out the damage, and got it frosted. Mutt ended up getting his share, which he gleefully wagged his tail.

"How was your day sweetie?" Dennis inquired. I told him well I'll tell you. It was pretty good except for the milk cow getting into the house; it took me and the kids to get her out. I was afraid she would leave a pile, of you know what on the floor. Guess that will teach me to keep the door shut. She sure is stubborn. "Oh sorry about that!" he said. He started to laugh. I gave him serious look and said, I don't think that's funny! He laughed all the harder. I couldn't help but to laugh myself. I never thought I would ever have to chase a cow out of my home. You think that's funny? You have to get the chicken out of the outhouse. It fell down the hole that stopped him laughing. "Oh no!" he said.

Dennis went out to see what he could do. He asked the kids "How long has she been in there?" Jill spoke up and said "Quite awhile." He went about tearing off the toilet seat, so he could put a ladder down into the hole. Sharlene asked "Is it going to die?" No honey, I said.

Denny said "It's got poo poo on it." Dennis stood there and gave it some thought. Then he said "Let's get that old wooden ladder. Maybe, just maybe, she will climb out by herself." The ladder was put into the hole and the chicken started to squawk and flapping her wings. She didn't get the idea that she needed to climb up the ladder. Chris said "She isn't doing it." Dad said "Just wait a while." Just a few minutes later she calmed down. They all looked at each other. They were all crowded around the outhouse.

Dad said very quietly "Shush, she's thinking about it. Get back we don't want to scare her, here she comes!" She got near the top of the ladder and started flapping her wings and came bursting out the door. All the kids started cheering.

Then the hen just started walking away looking very dignified. She didn't look to bad just mostly on her feet. Of course I was there watching the whole thing. I thought it was pretty funny. We were all standing around watching the hen prancing around. Mutt had been watching the whole thing. He thought he better check the hen out. He got close and sniffed at it then shook his head and sat down and looked at us, as if to say "pew." When Dennis finished putting the outhouse back in order, he came back into the house and said "Boy the excitement never ends around here."

Chapter 6

ALTHOUGH, HAYING TIME IS HARD work, it was the best time for all of us. The wonderful smell of fresh cut hay, we could feel the warm sunshine coming down on us, as we worked. After cutting the hay it had to be piled into small stacks which were called haycocks.

At times I would stop to rest; I would sit there watching my man pitching the hay. His dark hair shining in the sun and the muscles of his brown bareback, rippled as he moved so rhythmically. My heart felt so full of love, I thought it would burst, we love working together, and it gave us such a feeling of closeness. We felt very proud to stand and look at the evenly spaced haycocks in the field when we finished. Then it came time for the hay to be loaded onto the trailer and hauled to the barn. As each load was finished the children would climb aboard for the slow fun ride to the barn. With all the giggling and laughing you would think they were at a carnival. As the last load was being brought in, rain clouds started to gather. We really had to hurry now to beat the rain. It broke loose just as the last bit of hay was being put in. Exhausted and excited from the rushing, we laid on top of the pile of hay laughing. My man feeling a little devilish said "Just like in the movies," having said that, he rolled me head over heels down the side of the hay pile. I could do nothing but sit there and laugh as he came down after me.

Dennis looked at me and said "Boy you really got tanned."

Good, so did you, come on kids let's get something to eat. Are you hungry? I said.

Daddy said "Yeah! We are!"

The children would spend hours playing in the hay and never seem to tire of climbing the ladder and jumping off and landing deep into the hay.

During the last summer months we decided it would be nice to have my 16-year old, sister-in-law Mert, come stay with us for a while before school started. She could sleep on the couch, and would be good company for me during the long days. She and I always had gotten along really well. She adored the children and was so enthusiastic about everything.

We had to go into Dennis's parent's house in town to pick up his sister. When we got there we knocked and went in. Dad and Mom Smith were sitting in the living room. When they saw us, they just sat there looking at us like they didn't know us.

Dennis said "Well aren't you going to say hello? They were both staring at me. Dennis's Mom started getting a little upset.

I said it's me, Mom! Lola! I smiled and that did it.

Oh my goodness, please forgive me, I thought for a second, Dennis had a girlfriend. I know Dennis would never cheat on you." Mom got up and gave me a hug and Dennis's Dad was still staring at me, I smiled again and he said "Of course, I knew it was Lola."

On Saturday evening after we had all settled down to sleep we were disturbed by a clawing noise. Dennis immediately jumped up, turned on the light and grabbed the rifle that was still beneath the bed. Looking around he could not find anything. The noise had stopped. Just as he started to climb back into bed, Mert let out a scream and hollered "It's down here; it's down here on my bed. She screamed! There it is again." My husband grabbed the rifle again; he went down the stairs, forgetting in the excitement that he did not have his pants on.

With my head under the covers I could hear him stumbling into things in the darkness, and then the light was being turned on. Just then it dawned on me he was wearing nothing but his underwear. I grabbed his pants and took off down the stairs after him. Here we were, his sister sitting up in bed screaming and pointing here and there. My husband dashing around in his underclothes, trying to find it and I was following him around with his pants. He spotted it finally hiding behind the stove and taking careful aim, POW! There was one less grey digger! It was about the size of a rabbit, the biggest one we had ever seen. They were too smart for traps, so shooting them was the only way to get rid of them. We all crept up close to get a good look at it, just then Dennis got a funny look on his face and snatched his pants that I was still holding onto and he quickly put them on.

His sister ran and jumped into bed realizing she was just in her nighty. I just stood there still staring at the horrible looking thing on the floor. My husband put it outside in a box till morning. He would bury it before the children saw it. I couldn't believe the children slept through the whole episode.

Chapter 7

ONE EVENING WHEN DENNIS CAME home, he had a box of dynamite and caps, that he bought before coming home from work. I asked him, what on earth are you going to do with them?

He answered "I need to blow up some stumps, up on the top of the hill. We need to clear out stumps and trees, where the house will go." Then he looked at me with a little tiny smile, to see how I would react. With a look of concern on my face I said, isn't it dangerous?

"It could be if you're not careful." He said. Then he said "By the way your Uncle Milton is coming out this weekend. With a deep sigh I said, where on earth is he going to sleep?

"Don't worry Lola; he's a crusty old guy. He will probably sleep in the barn. As long as he has a couple bottle of ale, he's happy."

Well, I hope he's not in one of his teasing moods. It's his thing in life to pull something on me, I said with another deep sigh. Then I sat down at the table as I poured us both a cup of black coffee. I spoke up with concern, Dennis, have you done this before? I mean blowing things up?

He looked up at me with a rather superior look on his face "Of course, I have. By the way, where are the kids?" Dennis asked.

Little Darren is out front playing with his cars. He keeps trying to take them apart, without too much success. I looked out the window. He is so cute; he's already three years old. He sure looks like you, with his dark hair and brown eyes. Jill and Sharlene should be home soon, from the neighbors. Jolynn, Chris and Dennis Jr. are out in the old building just up the road. I told him.

Just then Jill came bursting through the door. "Mama! Mama! Guess what we saw!"

Okay, okay, just settle down.

Jill spoke up "We were at Hopper's place." She looked upset, her blue eyes started to tear up.

Sharlene spoke up "We saw Lily out by their rain barrel."

Yeah, Jill said. "Mama she had a little kitten and was drowning it.

I asked her why she was doing it," and she said "I like to see the bubbles."

Then she dropped the kitten and caught a baby chick and was going to do the same thing to the chick."

Sharlene cried, "I picked up the kitten and it was dead, Mama. Her green eyes were full of tears.

Jill continues, "We started yelling at her to stop. That's when her mom came out. When she saw what was going on, she grabbed Lily by the arm and swatted her butt and told her to go in to the house and she told us to go home."

"Well I can see that you both know it was very wrong. Just stay away from there for a while." Dennis said.

Just then we realize Jolynn, Chris and Dennis had come in and heard the whole conversation. We were all very still when Jolynn spoke up "Are they going to have a funeral?"

I said "Well maybe, but I don't want you there; I want you to stay away from their house for a while.

We don't go up there Mama, little six-year-old Chris said, shaking his head back and forth while five-year-old Dennis Jr. was doing the same but was quietly saying no, no.

Oh no, Darren is heading for the pond! I ran outside, as fast as I could. With everybody right behind me I caught him just in time.

No, no sweetie, stay away from the pond. He just looked at me and said "Car is broken" and threw the car a few feet towards the pond.

Whew, that was close! Daddy, you got to put a fence around the pond or something. It's too deep for such small kids. I said.

"Guess you're right, honey." He said

We better see what you two boys have been up to in the old building. "Wait for me daddy" called Jolynn.

They were gone for some time, and then Dennis came back in from the old building. I asked, well what have they been doing? Dennis had a grin on his face and said "You wouldn't believe it. They are making a hide out at the far end of, the chicken coop.

Chapter 8

One evening Dennis was talking about the work he was doing to clear some of the land up above.

I asked him how his hands were because several days ago, he was clearing out the scotch bloom around the cabin. His hands had broken out in a rash and were starting to blister, that night. The doctor gave him some purple medicine to soak them in morning and at night. He went to work regardless. I was still concerned about him.

He answered "My hands are all right, don't worry." Needless to say he had to stay away from the scotch bloom, but he had gotten rid of most of it, before his hands started breaking out.

Early Saturday morning an old car pulled up beside the cabin. I went out to see who it was. A tall man got out, I was startled! He was about the ugliest guy I have ever seen. I went quickly back into the house. Dennis! Dennis! He came over by the door and looked out, and started laughing. About that time the man reached up under his chin and pulled off a mask! It was my Uncle Milton!!

Hi sweetie, aren't you going to give your Uncle Milton a hug?

No, you old nut, you scared me, I told him. By this time Dennis and Milton were laughing like crazy.

All right you guys come get breakfast and get to work. I said with a somewhat relief on my face.

"Oh come on Lola, just having a little fun." Milton said with a grin on his face.

I muttered, Yeah, Yeah! I turned my back to him, but couldn't help smiling. We all started laughing.

While I got the kids up for breakfast, Dennis and Milton discussed about where they would start blowing stumps. The kids, who missed nothing, all started hollering, can we come!

No, I said raising my voice. Although I thought I wouldn't mind watching it myself.

Please! They all coaxed.

Well hey Honey, if they stay far enough away, they could watch, with you keeping an eye on them. Are you kids listening? Dad warned them! They all nodded.

All right come here kids, when the guys are ready, we will go up and watch them. But first we need to do chores. Jill, you bring a couple buckets of water, Sharlene, you help me with the dishes, Jolynn, feed the chickens. Chris and Dennis, you go put some hay out for the calves. But, first bring down your dirty clothes. Darren, you can stay with Mama. Okay, gang let's go!

Twenty minutes later they were back in the house, looking excited. Well that was fast. Daddy might not be ready yet, but I guess we could go up and watch anyway, I said. I took a hold of Darren hand and we headed out. Although Darren thought he was too big to hold onto Mom's hand, so he took off with the other kids. When we arrived they were still digging around a large stump. The neighbor man Ted, had come over and was taking turns helping, because we only had two shovels.

The kids all ran over to see what they were doing. "Hey kids, now look I want you to go over to that big log way over there, it will be a little while yet." Dad said pointing in the direction of the log.

As we were all getting settled, I noticed Milton was waiting for his turn to dig. I also noticed he was wandering off into the woods and something was hanging out of his back pocket. I guessed what he was up to. He's going to scare the kids. I worried it might be too scary for them. I gathered the kids close and lowered my voice and told the kids that Uncle Milton might be sneaking up to scare you with a scary mask, so when he does just yell "Hi Milton" don't be scared it's not real. Okay! Sure enough I could see him coming up behind us. Here he comes, I said.

He jumped out from a bush and went Grrrr! The kids jumped and turned around and hollered "Hi Milton". He made a couple of more growling noises then said "Oh nuts" then took off his mask and asked "Didn't it scare you at all? "No" the kids yelled.

Dennis Jr. jumped forward and said "We saw the mask, down at the house. Ha! Ha!"

Then we were all laughing. I should have never worried. "Hey Milton, get over here and stop fooling around," Dennis said. It was time to blow the stumps. "Okay! Everyone get behind the log now! Dennis hollered. We were already behind the log peeking over when there came the three guys running like crazy and jumping over the log with us. Hold your ears kids!

There were a few tense moments, as we waited for the explosion and then **Boom**! It was amazing the stump went straight up in the air about four feet, came down and landed right back in the same hole it came out of, which was now a big, big hole. We all stood up and Darren started to cry and the rest the kids were holding their ears. The men stood there a few minutes looking at it.

"Well, we sure as hell used enough dynamite!" Dennis said.

They walked over to the stump. Milton said "I sure didn't figure on pulling it out of a same hole, as it came out of."

"The tractor will take care of that" replied Dennis

Come on kids, I said. But they were already running over to see the big hole. Ted was kind of laughing. Then he said "You never know do you?" I got to go guys. Good luck!"

As the kids and I headed back to the cabin the kids were talking;

Jill said "I'm glad I'm not a guy." Sharlene spoke up and said "me too!" Jolynn piped up and said "I would like to blow up stumps."

Chris added "It was sure loud."

Dennis Jr. "It was really cool." Darren was looking over my shoulder and said "cool."

While the kids were having lunch we heard another **Boom**! The kids looked up said "There goes another stump."

Chapter 9

LATER DENNIS CAME DOWN TO the house for some lunch. I asked him, is Milton coming down for lunch? No, he said he wasn't hungry. Milton told me he found a wild cherry tree and he got a good witching stick, so he's going to go witching for water, while I'm hauling the stumps out of the way.

The kids wanted to go watch. I told them they could if they stayed out of the way. Darren asked "Me too?" We'll look out for him Mom" Jill said. "Okay." I sent some lunch up for Milton with Dennis.

After I cleaned up after lunch, I thought I would go up and see how things were going. When I got there Milton was chasing the kids around with the witching stick. They were having a great time. Darren was riding on Milton's neck. It was a wonderful day for kids.

There was a nice warm breeze with the sun shining down. I could smell the fresh dirt, which the guys had dug up around the stumps. The breeze brought the green pine smell of the forest. I just sat down and listened to the children laughing and wondered how long Milton would keep up with our energetic kids.

Milton was well into his 60s, about 5 foot 11 inches, with broad shoulders and walked with a swagger. He was some character! It wasn't long before he sat down on the ground and gathered them around and decided to explain what he was trying to do, I listened in.

See this stick; he said it's like a Y. Now then if you hold the top part of the Y and let the long part of the stick out in front of you and walk very slowly, it will tip down to the ground and show you where you can find water! "Like this." He said as he stood up and walked slowly around.

"How's it going Milton?" Dennis hollered "Not so good, it will take some time." said Milton. The kids didn't look too happy. "That's okay kids we'll keep trying, "said Dad.

That evening Dennis asked Milton, "Any sign of water yet?"

"Not yet, I'm afraid I have to get home tomorrow." Milton told Dennis.

"Well, maybe I'll give it a try!" said Dennis "Us kids can help Daddy" said Sharlene "We'll see" said Dad.

Chapter 10

I<small>T WAS REAL QUIET AFTER</small> Milton left that Sunday. But it wasn't very long before we had more company. I didn't know if our relatives would be critical or think we were nuts or would have liked to try something like this themselves.

Maybe they'll surprise me!

My sister and her husband and two boys came that Sunday. My younger sister wanted to see everything, she was quite intrigued. Each weekend it seemed like we had company.

Both of our parents were like us, they only saw the potential. All four of them couldn't get over how much better food tasted, cooked on a wooden stove. Both our mothers loved the old cook stove; it reminded them of long ago. Our mothers didn't get along very well. They very seldom came at the same time, only at family gatherings.

Dennis and I both had a few brothers and sisters. I had two sisters and two brothers, Dennis had three sisters and three brothers. Needless, to say we had quite a few nephews and nieces. They loved coming to see us, because they had plenty of room to run around. Of course, we had to put a stop to playing in the hay in the barn.

Our families were good about bringing something for lunch or dinner. That really helped seeing as how there was so many of us. They got a kick out of using the outhouse. But some of them didn't like using the outhouse.

Dennis enjoyed showing off the old barn. He had a good time showing the guys around the place. One time the guys came down from the barn. Dennis asked me "Hey Lola, I didn't see the milk cow."

"Oh yeah I forgot to tell you, Ted (the neighbor) decided to sell her. "Oh I guess we will miss the milk" Dennis stated. Not really, we really didn't get much milk from her; I guess she dried up or something. I thought to myself, I'm glad she's gone, dumb cow!

Of course, Dennis had to ask Ted about the cow out of curiosity. Ted told him that she was just too much trouble, because she kept wandering off, so I sold her. I muttered, tell me about it!

"What?" Dennis asked

Oh nothing, I replied.

Curriers (on my dad's side of the family) were a bunch of characters. They like to have a good time. Having fun was their thing in life. They also like to tease! I don't know why they like to tease me; I guess they like my reaction when they teased me. I had to learn, as the saying goes "take it with a grain of salt." But my salt was getting low, I sighed a lot. But they were funny.

If they came to visit and stayed late, we would have a bonfire. They would always bring along their harmonicas and guitars. We would all attempt to sing old-time songs. The kids got to stay up for a while longer. We had hot dogs and marshmallows at the bonfire. At least one of my uncles had to get up and dance a jig. The kids would laugh, so hard they would be rolling on the ground.

To my surprise our kids decided to get into the party and started to jig along to the music, even little Darren. Don't know how come I deserve such wonderful kids! Of course, their mom had to get into the act! Wow! What fun!

Mutt was racing around, barking and howling. I think he liked the music too. It was time for the children to go to bed. When they were saying their prayers, they thanked God for the good time they had. Maybe next time they could stay up again, they knew I was listening.

Most of my mother's family was back east. I had only met two of her brothers, although she had quite a large family. She probably thought my dad's family was kooky. But she is a good sport.

Dennis's folks, like a good many people most of their families are still back east too. Both of our parents were up to a challenge. I guess that's why my parents moved from one place to another during all my childhood. Yeah, that's where I got it from; I called it an adventure. Dennis was sure up to it!

Chapter 11

ONE DAY I WAS BUSY in the house when I heard the kids hollering I went outside. Jolynn, Chris, and Dennis Jr., were coming down the road from the barn.

Dennis Jr. "Mama! Mama! Hurry, hurry then he turned and yelled at the other kids!

Chris – "It's not following us!"

Jolynn – "Boy it was big!"

I said – "Whoa, what's going on?"

Dennis Jr. – "It's a big bear, mom."

"All right start from the beginning" I said

Jolynn – "We were by the fence line and this big brown bear was looking around the fence."

Chris – "We stayed on our side of the fence, like you told us.

Jolynn – "We stayed real quite like you told us too.

Dennis Jr. – "It didn't see us."

Chris – "We waited till it went away."

"Which way did it go?" Oh Lord where is Darren? I asked.

Dennis Jr. – "He wanted to stay in our hideout."

You kids stay in the house. You hear? I ran out to the hideout and found Darren just as he was coming out of the building.

Darren – "What's the matter mama?"

Come here sweetie, I picked him up and headed back to the cabin. I told him, we need to stay close to the cabin.

Darren – Why?

To keep you safe, I told him

"Why?"

Because Daddy will be home soon, I gave a quick look around, saw nothing like a bear.

After we got back into the cabin, I told the kids to come sit down. Now you remember that I told you, that even if wild animals seem tame, you stay away from them. They can still hurt you.

"We know mama." Jolynn said.

Was the dog with you? I asked. "No, he was with Darren." Dennis Jr. answered. Then he said "He's right behind you mom."

Alright you kids stay in the house and play games or something. Daddy will be home soon and he will check out where the bear went. We want to make sure you kids are safe.

When Dennis got home, all the kids started telling him about the bear, he asked a lot of question about it. It was still pretty light out yet, so he went out to get his 270 rifle out of the pickup truck. He told me he was going to get the neighbor Ted to go with him. I said you're not going to shoot him are you? "No just a safety measure." He said.

The kids and I played games and waited for Dennis to come back. Finally, a little after dark he came back. Well? I said. Dennis told me, "It got too dark for us to see anything, but I don't think the bear will be back for awhile. Ted told me he comes around about once a month. Ted thinks he is pretty old, because from what he has heard, he has been around for years. Pretty sure he is the same one. He has never really bothered anyone, but we will keep an eye out."

The next morning it was time to feed the chickens. I took the kids out with me; I also took Mutt so he could tell me, if there was any strange thing hanging around. The boys went back to their hide out in back of the building. Mutt went with them, after he sniffed the area. I wondered if he was all that good at protecting us. He wasn't very big. I guess he didn't smell anything unusual.

Jill said "Mom what is wrong with those two chicken? Sharlene said their making a funny noise."

Jolynn said "Yeah, they are clucking."

Yeah! Their starting to lay, I said. "Lay what?" Jolynn asked.

EGGS!

"Where are they?" Jill asked.

Their under the chickens, just reach under it and you will find an egg, I said.

The girls did not like the idea at all; the boys came out of their hide out and wanted to know what was going on. Look boys we have two eggs, I told them. Darren asked, "Where did they come from?" Jill said, "From the chicken, they laid them. Then Sharlene said "They were sitting on them." Then she giggled. Pretty soon we will have a lot of eggs, and also later on we will have some baby chicks"

Mutt was sitting there tilting his head from side to side. I think he was a little confused, why we were taking his eggs. He is minding better and he seems to think the chickens are his to take care of. Too bad he can't collect eggs. He's turning out to be a pretty smart dog.

CHICKEN COOP   HIDE OUT

Chapter 12

LAUNDRY DAY IS SOMETHING THAT I did not look forward too. Water needed to be hauled and heated then more water hauled for rinsing. I had a washer that had a spin tub for the rinsing, thank goodness.

Dennis had fixed a place on the floor in the back part of the cabin which worked out fine for the spin tub. The thing is it took most of the day to get the washing done. Then I would have to hang the clothes on the line, if it was nice, I would hang them outside. If it was raining Dennis set up a line for me inside the cabin. At least we had clean clothes.

The kids really get dirty living here. Bathing is a whole different "Ball Game." The girls had a certain day of the week and the boys another day of the week. Sometimes the boys would get so dirty they got another bath day. I got a bright idea! The pond wasn't all that deep. I had the kids strip down to their under pants and play in the pond. I was glad it was summer. Of course Mama had to get in too, with her bathing suit on. It worked out pretty good. Lucky Dennis used the shower at work.

It was a beautiful day; I had one window open to let the cool breeze in. It was a calm, peaceful day. We didn't have a T.V. and the radio was off. The kids and I were sitting around the table playing board and card games.

Sharlene said in a quiet voice, "Mom there's a dragon fly in here, as she looked out of the corner of her eyes. I looked up sure enough it was over by the cupboard. I said, sit still, don't move. To my amazement it came over to where we were and was checking each of us out. The kids sat real still, the only thing moving was their eyes. Then it just flew out the window. We had a good laugh! Jill thought it was real pretty. Jolynn thought maybe she could catch one. The boys were still laughing and pretending they were dragonflies, so much for a quite day.

That evening after the little ones were all settled in bed I thought I would sit outside. I wanted to enjoy the night air. Dennis was going over some papers. The stars were out and the air was warm and felt like velvet on my skin. The moon was reflecting on the pond, the evening was so lovely.

A short time later Dennis came to join me. "Mind if I join you honey?" he said. Of course not, I replied with a smile. He said "Just look at those beautiful stars. This is so nice to be here with you, sweetheart." We don't get much quite time do we?" I love you honey, I told him. Then he said "I know but it is nice to hear you say it. I love you too. Do you think we're doing the right thing? It's pretty hard on you." He said with a look of concern on his face.

Oh I'm alright, I worry about the children but they are sure learning a lot about nature, I replied. He moved closer to me and put his arm around me and kissed me on the forehead. "It will get better." He said. I answered, I sure hope so. We grew quiet and enjoyed the evening.

Mutt came up to us and sat down and wanted us to pet him. "He has become quite a dog. He is really trying to impress us. He has been catching all kinds of rodents and leaving them on the door step instead of eating them. He herds the chickens back if they get to far away. I can't get over how he tries to watch over everything. He's been so good; I've been letting him stay in the house if he wants too. I saw him sniffing all around the cabin just after dark, just checking things out before bed time.

As Dennis was petting and scratching Mutts head. He said "See I told you he was a smart dog." I don't know, I think he might be possessed by a spirit of some kind. I said, with a puzzled look on my face. Dennis said, "Oh come on let's go to bed, come on Mutt." I told Dennis, well it could be possible, and people get possessed sometimes. I got up and followed them into the house.

Chapter 13

The next day Jill came into the house all excited and said "Mom, I think you should come out to the boy's hide out." I said, as we hurried out to the building where they had their hide out, What's wrong? Jill answered, "I don't know Mutt is acting kind of strange."

The far end of the building had a dirt floor where Mutt was digging like crazy. He was trying to dig up what looked like a dirty old smelly rag of some sort.

The kids were all talking at the same time. "He won't stop digging mom! There is something in there. You think it's a dead person? No it isn't! I get to tell dad. What is it mom?"

Alright calm down! I said as I pulled Mutt back from the hole. What is it boy, what did you find? I asked him. I pulled on the smelly old rag and I saw something else. It looked like some kind of "BONE."

Chris hand me the shovel. I told him. The kids grew quiet and looked like they were holding their breath.

Mom! Mom! Daddy's home! They all ran out to get him. Oh, good I'm glad he is home, I thought, it's probably just a dead animal. Dennis came in with the kids crowded around him. "What's going on?" He asked looking puzzled.

The kids all started in to explain to their Dad what was going on. "Mutt found something! It could be a dead body! We found a bone! Two bones!"

Darren jumped into his dad's arms looking a little scared. "Now kids it's just a dead animal that someone buried. Let's take a look" He said as he set Darren down and took the shovel from me.

Dennis looked at me and said "Why so excited?"

I don't know Dennis, Mutt was really excited. You know how he is. I said doing my best to look calm. Dennis looked at me and rolled his eyes. He started digging and found more bones.

"Yep, it's some kind of animal, wait a minute there is something down deeper? It's some kind of metal." He said. He kept digging. It looks like it might be a box! Mutt was sitting there panting; I could swear he had a smile on his face.

Sure enough it was a fairly good size box. Dennis got down on his knees and pulled it out of the hole. It looked heavy. There a latch but no lock. Dennis said "Ok, let's clean it off and take it to the house. I looked at Mutt he was wagging his tail and jumping around. I looked at him and wondered [What kind of a dog are you?] We gathered around the table while Dad examined the box, it was sixteen by ten by eight inches. Wow! It was rusted shut so Dennis pried it loose. Then he waited and said "Are you ready?" We all yelled "Yes."

All right here we go, inside was something wrapped in a package and a beautiful carved wooden box. We opened the wooden box first; it had some expensive looking jewelry and a paper??? There was a paper that was all rolled up, as I unrolled it, it was a letter, and it was kind of hard to read. This is want it said:

To whoever finds this I leave my fortune. I am alone in this old world. Greta my dear wife has gone to heaven. If anyone finds this, I hope they will put it to good use.

Otherwise good old mother earth will claim it. This was buried when my dear dog Carl passed away.

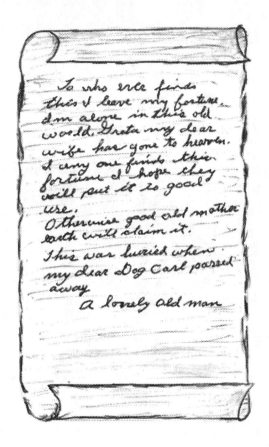

We all sat there feeling sad, about the lonely old man. I told you Dennis, I think Mutt is physic, and he's possessed by Carl! From now on his name will be "Carl." Carl looked up and wagged his tail and gave me another smile. Dennis smiled and said "It's making a believer out of me."

"Ok, let's see what is in the package. Are you ready?" Dennis said. Everyone hollered, YES! The package looked like it was wrapped in very old paper and then some sort of oil parchment.

When we open the oil parchment we saw, there were two stacks of paper money. Also in the bottom of the box there was a pile of gold coins. The kid's started jumping around and laughing. I had a hard time catching my breath. Dennis stared in disbelief; he started counting the paper money. He slapped his hand to his forehead and held it there in disbelieve, the kids and I did the same thing. Dennis finished counting the money "A hundred thousand dollars! Woo WE!! Dennis looked over at the kids and asked "How many gold coins are there?"

The kids stacked the coins up and they told him there are fifty coins Dad. I couldn't even guess their value. Inside the wood box there was a pile of jewelry. I told the kids to hand me the jewelry; the kids had already sorted the jewelry all out. There were necklaces, rings, bracelets, tie clips, cufflinks, money clips, and brooches. I told Dennis this looks like pretty expensive jewelry! Lonely man and Greta must have had quite a social life or inherited all this. I guessed, with a somewhat puzzled look on my face.

What are we going to do? I think having the lonely man's letter we may be able to keep it. Don't you think Dennis? Dennis had a look of concern on his face. He said "Let's talk to our lawyer and see where we stand. In the mean time we can put it in a safety deposit box in the bank." Great idea! I said. The kids were real still, looking back and forth from dad to me. Jill spoke up, "Does that mean we can't spend it?" I told her, maybe in time.

Chapter 14

I WISH WE KNEW MORE about lonely man. I hate calling him lonely man. I said. Anyone have an idea what we could call him?

The kids all had ideas of what to call him from Old man, Rich man, Stranger, Angel, Lone man, Lone Stranger and many other names.

Let's have daddy decide, he brought Carl home (aka Mutt), I said. We all agreed he should make the decision. He said with a deep sigh. "Let me see the list. What do you all think about the "Lone Stranger?" It sounds like Lone Ranger." We all agreed. "Lone Stranger it is then." He said. "Now kids this is to be kept a secret, until we find out more about it. I mean it! All of you raise your right hand," he said. They all raised their hands and had very serious looks on their faces, even little Darren. Dad said "Repeat after me, I swear I will keep the Lone Stanger fortune a secret." The kids all repeated after him, while looking at us with big round eyes.

We very seldom kept things from the children. We just hope they can keep this quite till we get it figured out. Darren piped up and said, "Who is the Lone Ranger?" That will take some explaining, since we don't have T.V. here.

The next day I got a babysitter and I met Dennis after he got off work. I told him I thought we would have to get two safety deposit boxes at the bank. I had bought a satchel to carry the money into the bank. I carried the Lone Stranger's letter in my purse. I felt like we were doing something illegal. I asked Dennis, we aren't doing anything illegal are we? He answered, "No that's why we are going to talk to Ed [our lawyer]. Did you make an appointment? "Yes it's late, but he said he would wait.

We have known Edward Lukas for a few years. He was a tall man with a nice build and very good looking. He was getting a little gray around the temples, he reminded me of John Wayne! We have become very good friends, really a great guy.

"Well let's get to it." Dennis said as he looked at me and smiled and said "Ok Bonnie let's load up the loot." I looked at him and winked and said "Ok Clyde let's do it." After we got our loot into the bank, we went straight to the lawyer, Edward Lukas's office. After we told him how we found the fortune, he read the letter. Ed told us he knew a jeweler that is very honest and reliable. Since it is so late you can make an appointment to see him tomorrow. In fact he can tell you if the bills are counterfeit or not and give you an appraisal on the gold coins and jewelry. He then told us, "I will do some research to see if there has been a robbery in the amount of the fortune, or anything that I can find out. We only have the name of his wife. I doubt if we can find out anything about the couple. It appears that this was done a long time ago. I have to tell you, I love a good challenge, and a mystery!" This is one heck of a mystery! Dennis told him "Great, we sure will keep in touch."

Ed told us to take the jewels and the gold coins and have them evaluated. If the bills is counterfeit just tell them you found it and that is all. You may have too forfeite all of them. Let me know what you find out. He gave us direction to the Jeweler, where we could have this done.

We told Ed, "We can't get to the bank till tomorrow." Alright how about two o'clock tomorrow? I turned to Dennis and asked him if he could get off work early. He said "Yes, I think I can. Ed gave us the jeweler's card, if we couldn't make it, to give the jeweler a call to let him know, if you can't make it.

Dennis told him "Great, we will keep in touch." We were both so excited. Oh Dennis, is this really happening? I asked. He replied "It seems like a dream. As we were driving home I said What if! Dennis said, "No, don't go there; we could drive ourselves crazy doing what **ifs**." Your right, one day at a time, I agreed.

Chapter 15

IN THE AFTERNOON WE WENT to see the jeweler. We asked the clerk if we could see the owner, we have appointment with him. The young lady said "Oh yes, you must be the Smith's, he's expecting you," as she pointed the direction to his office. She took us back to his office. Mr. Gloss, this is the Smith's, your next appointment. We all shook hands. "Please call me Ben." He said. Dennis said "Call us Dennis and Lola, it's nice to meet you!

Mr. Ben Gloss was a delightful looking man, with a round face, he had spectacles on his little stubby nose and was about five foot nine. Ben motioned Dennis to put the heavy satchel on his large deck. "Well now let's see what we have here.

Ed told me about this over the phone. Please sit down. It sounds most intriguing." As he opened up the satchel and was taking a look at what was inside, he became more and more excited. "Gee ho sa fat! I never thought it would be so large! Let's take a look at those bills." He said.

After about five minute, he said "Well the money are not counterfeit, but the good news is these are Silver Certificates. The silver certificates were issued to save money on expensive bank note paper. This note featured a smaller size than its predecessor and a bank design that many people thought was counterfeit. They have a unique "Funny Looking" design on the back, seldom seen and highly collectible. These were printed in 1928. That would make them thirty years old. It doesn't give us a clue how this person come to have them. Maybe Ed will come up with something."

Ben took off his glasses and wiped them off and said "By the way Ed would like to know if he could have a look at the jewelry later, maybe it will give him some clues. He might be able to track them down. I must tell you this is going to take some time. If you could wait, I can take some pictures of everything, I will get some real close ups. I can give the pictures to Ed, and that way you can put everything back in the bank." Dennis said "That's ok with us." Then Ben said "I would like you to stay while I do this. I will tell my girl Friday not to disturb us. I want to check things out in the front office, so we won't be disturbed. Can you lay out the jewelry and coins, so we get real close pictures of everything?" We agreed and told Ben we would be glad too.

When he came back we had it all laid out! "Good Good," he said with an excited smile and a gleam in his eye. Then he picked up the wooden box and said "You know this wooden box, might have some real value too." He started taking pictures, not only the front but also the back of everything. While he did this he kept talking. He said "Guess you can tell how excited I am, it's been some time since I've seen anything like this. I can give Ed a copy of the pictures, it might help him, is that ok with you?" We both nodded.

Ben continued "It's a good bet you will become very rich, but you must be patient, this will take time. I must be very careful about who we let know about this, but I have a wide variety of connections, I can trust," as he winked at us. About an hour later he had finished taking all of the pictures, and logging all of the items. Ben then said "Ok, you can pack everything up and take it back to the bank, but be very careful, make sure no one is following you."

We then packed up our loot and the letter. We shook hands and headed to the bank, and got it all put back into the safety deposit boxes. I looked at the deposit box keys and thought; I still don't feel this is real. Dennis looked at me and knew what I was thinking. Then said "I know honey, I know." We couldn't help but hug each other. We didn't what to jinx our good fortune.

As we quietly drove home, I finally spoke up and said how come we are not more excited? Dennis thought for awhile then said "Maybe it's because it is such a mystery." Well I guess we'll have to wait and see what they come up with, I replied.

The next day I had a hard time trying to keep my mind on every day things that needed to be done. The Lone Stranger thing kept nagging at me, what if this, what if that.

Chapter 16

I DECIDED TO TAKE THE kids and walk up to get the mail. The mail box was about one eighth of a mile, with wooded areas along both side of the road. The kids all liked going for the mail. They loved running ahead and hiding in the woods and jumping out and trying to scare me. Of course, I had to act like they did scare me, after fifteen times, I told them to stop.

While we were standing alongside of the road at the mail box, a beat up old pickup truck pulled into our road. It stopped at the old shack on the right side of the road. I didn't think anyone lived there. I told the kids; let's wait here by the mail box for a minute. I only saw two mail boxes including ours. I didn't think they owned the property, it wasn't anyone I knew.

The guy on the passenger side got out and turned around and looked at us. He was about five foot nine with long dirty looking hair, squinty eyes, and dirty raggedy clothes. He reached into the pickup to help a woman out of the pickup. She was very stout and also looked dirty and had way too much makeup on. Mean while the driver got out and was taking a couple of duffel bags out of the bed of the truck. He looked up at us and what I thought was an evil smile which showed his rotten teeth. His hair was long, and he had a shaggy beard. He was taller than the other one but was heavier with a pot belly also long stringy hair like the other two.

I told the kids to stay close. They knew something wasn't right, so they did as I said. We started walking along the opposite side of the road. The driver started coming toward us and said "What are you doing here?" I didn't answer and kept going. He yelled and said "Hey I'm talking to you, are all those brats yours." We kept walking a little faster. The other two came over beside him and started laughing. The woman said "Did we scare you honey?" She said it with a snide look on her face. I told the kids to run home, as fast as, you can.

I waited till the kids got around the curve in the road. I started to shake; no way I was going to let them get at my kids. Mutt stood there stiff legged with his teeth bared and was growling low. It was then we heard a truck coming down the road. I knew it had to be Ted. The three of them looked at each other and walked over behind their pickup, they were whispering.

Ted stopped his truck and got out. He looked very intimidating, with his bright red hair and bushy red beard. He had a slight snarl on his face. He said "Alright what is going on here?" The driver said "Oh, nothing we just thought we would rest here for the night." Just then Ted pulled back the side of his jacket and showed a badge. My mouth dropped open; I didn't know he was a deputy sheriff!

Then Ted said "I think not, you better move on." He walked over to the pickup and looked inside and removed two rifles and a pistol. He then emptied the ammunition from all of them and put the bullets in his pocket. "Now Git!" He told them.

They couldn't get in their pickup fast enough. They threw their duffle bags in their truck and got turned around and left in a hurry. When they were gone the kids jumped out of Ed's truck. I was so surprise to see them, getting out of the back of his truck. All the kids were yelling things like, yeah Ted scared them, they were mean, and yeah they were ugly too. Then they saw Ted's badge. Jill said "Are you a sheriff?" Ted kind of laughed and said "Not really, take a look." They all looked puzzled. I told them "It's not real!" He said "It comes in handy sometimes."

I can't thank you enough Ted, I had no idea what they were up to. He replied, "Well it's not the first time we've had squatters trying to move in, I'm just glad I caught them. That shack should be torn down. These people give us nothing but trouble. There is no electricity or plumbing. I don't understand why anyone would want to stay here. Would you like a ride home?" The kids all jumped into the back of his truck. I laughed and said, I guess that's your answer.

When Dennis got home the kids were all over him, telling him what happened. He just said "So Ted has a fake badge huh?" Then he kind of laughed. Sure glad everyone is all right." I wonder if Ted would like to go up there and tear that shack down. I think I'll go up and thank him for what he did."

The next Saturday that's what they did. When Dennis came back from tearing down the shack, he had someone with him. I went out to see who it was. It was my brother Danny, he came over and gave me a big hug and said "Hi sis!" I was so glad to see him. Then he said with a twinkle in his eye "Your old man got me to help with that old shack, just a couple whacks, and the darn thing fell over." Dennis said with a grin "Now all we have to do is clean up the mess. We couldn't have done it without you Dan."

Danny was about five foot nine, with wavy light brown hair and real pretty blue eyes. He stayed for dinner after Dennis showed him around the place. It was really nice talking about old times, and then he had to leave but said he would be back, if I don't get arrested by that deputy Ted. Then we all laughed, Dennis had told him what happened the other day.

Chapter 17

ANOTHER LAUNDRY DAY, THANK GOODNESS Dennis brought our dryer out of storage; it made laundry day a lot easier. I was folding laundry when Dennis arrived home from work. I looked out the window, there was something going on. The kids were all gathered around their dad. They always looked forward to daddy coming home. I went back to folding clothes when they all came in. Jill said "Daddy has something for you mom, look look!" I turned around and there he was holding a bouquet of roses, with a very pleased look on his face.

He said "Remember when we lived in town, every spring I would get you daffodils, well you deserve more." He held out the roses to me. "Oh, honey that is so sweet, thank you." I said and gave him a big kiss.

The kids were as pleased as their dad. They were a part of everything. I said "What is the special occasion?" Dennis said "There is no special occasion. I told them we all should let you know how much we appreciate you." They all said together "We love you momma!"

I reached behind me and took a folded towel and wiped the tears from my eyes. I said "Help me put these clothes away and I will fix you a special dinner for no reason, except I love you all. It was the first time we had flowers on the table since we moved here. Dennis and I looked at each other over dinner and smiled. We are so proud of our little family.

Ed our lawyer called and wanted to know if it would be alright if Ben and he could come out on Saturday. They would like to look at the place where the treasure was found. They are hoping to find some kind of clue to the Lonesome Stranger. I told him "Yes they sure could." I was getting excited again.

I told Dennis about the call. I thought I had better get some groceries so I could have enough for lunch and dinner. I was surprised things were so involved. I didn't get much sleep that night. Dennis didn't seem to have any trouble at all. He seemed pretty calm about the whole thing.

My mind was jumping all around. Let's see I'll have fried chicken, corn on the cob, mashed potatoes and gravy, biscuits, salad and apple pie. Oh, I don't know. Maybe there is something they can't eat. Oh, I'm getting so confused. Next thing I knew it was morning. It was really hard to keep my mind on things, because I had so many things to do before Saturday.

Saturday finally rolled around, Ed and Ben arrived at ten a.m. We went out to meet them. They looked all around. Ben said "Man you sure got your work cut out for you." Ed said "I can't wait to look around, I want to see everything. I brought a real old map with me. Maybe I can figure out how things might have changed." Dennis was more than happy to show them around. Ed turned around and said "Are you coming Ben?" Ben answered "yeah sure." Then he turned to me, Ed is getting really possessed with this whole thing. I want to talk with you later ok? Sure no problem, I said. I watched them head up to the top of the property.

Of course the kids wanted to know what was going on. So I told them, we are trying to find out who the Lone Stanger could be. They asked if they could go along. I told them, they are very busy. Maybe when they come back down here you can watch, but stay out of the way.

After a while we saw them go by the window. Ed was carrying his old map; Ben seemed to be taking notes. I went out to see if they would like some lunch. I told them I have some homemade stew and biscuits when they were ready. The kids had just finished their lunch, when the guys came in and sat down. They really seemed to be enjoying their lunch. Ben said "This is really good Lola." I said, thank-you Ben, the wood fire gives it a good flavor.

As they finished eating, Ed asked "Would you two mind if Ben and I did some digging out in the building where you found the treasure?" We said it would be ok by us. Dennis and Ed started out toward the building. Ben held back to talk to me. He told me that he had almost finished appraising the jewelry. With a very serious look on his face he said "All of it is very old and so far it is very valuable. I mean you could send all six of your children threw collage. You might want to pick out something for yourself. When and if you decide you would like to sell it, I could do that for you.

As I told you before I have a good many contacts. "I stood there with a studded look on my face. Ben said, "Unless Ed finds something illegal, but I don't think that will be likely." I had a hard time finding my voice. Ben waited patiently waiting for my response. Finally I managed to say "I can't tell you how grateful we are that you and Ed are taking such an interest and putting so much time into it.

Ben responded "No need to worry, even if thing don't work out, Ed and I will have enough to write a book. Of course, we will need your permission. Ed told me he was going to write everything down as we go along and keep you informed so don't you worry Lola. We all are going to come out of this very wealthy people, one way or another." I couldn't help myself; I gave him a big hug, he grinned and blushed, and left.

Chapter 18

I WENT OUT TO THE chicken coop to see if the kids were behaving themselves. I was amazed how much of the dirt floor the men had dug up. They had moved the boy's hideout to make room for them to dig. They stopped and looked up at me. Did you find anything? I said.

Dennis said "Just an old boot and a couple of whiskey bottles."

Ed said "I think this used to be an old trail though here."

Ben said "Yeah we found some burnt wood, could have been a camp fire. Ed straightens up and said "Well we aren't going to get anywhere this way; we would have to get a bulldozer. I really don't think we're going to find anything worthwhile. Let's fill up the hole. "Ok, by me." Ben said.

"Well you know we didn't check over in the corner." Dennis said. Ed looked over at the corner and said "Let's give it a try, who knows what there might be there. I piped up, as long as you guys are willing to do the digging!

The dog Carl has been laying there whining. There must be something under the dirt. Ed had a very thoughtful look on his face and said let's try to figure this out. He buried his treasure right over there. It looks like the remains of a camp fire over here. Maybe he died here by the fire, right where Carl has been trying to tell us. So just maybe his remains are here!"

Ben said "I don't know if I want to do this. Do you really think his remains are here?"

Dennis said "You aren't getting spooked are you Ben?"

"I tell you, little Carl is making a believer out of me! I hope Lone Stanger is here. I don't think he would be very far down according to the campfire." Ed said. The three guys were standing there looking at one another. Then Dennis said "Ok, guys let's do this."

The kids and I were standing back out of the way. I didn't know if the kids should see this. If they should find a skeleton, I didn't want it to scare them. I told the kids to come help me with the chores. They didn't want to but we headed out for the barn. I heard Chris and Denny talking. They were wondering if they would get there hideout back. (Of course we had to give Dennis Jr. the nick name Denny).

Meanwhile, the guys were still digging. When we came back from the barn, the kids took off running. I couldn't stop the kids from going back into the chicken coop, leaving Darren and I, bringing up the rear. Just before Darren and I got to the door, Jill came running out. She said "Hurry mom, daddy found something." So much for keeping it from the kids!

By now the guys were digging with their hands. They found what looked like a leg bone. Ben said "Oh god Ed! I think I found his skull!" "Hurrah" Ed said. Dennis seemed very calm, compared to Ben and Ed. He said "I think I found his foot and what looks like his other boot."

Ed took a deep breath and tried to calm down then said "Ok, let' get something to lay these bones on. Dennis said "Lola, go get a sheet." I ran to the cabin to find an old sheet. My heart was really pounding. When I got back they found more bones. It didn't take long to find the rest of the Lone Stranger. They kept looking through the dirt thinking there just might find something else.

Ed said "Be careful guys." Ed started looking at the bones. He was talking all the while "I guess he didn't go to the dentist. So that's out. He hasn't been here very long, maybe twenty years or so. There are some fragments of his clothing; his boots are pretty much gone.

Just then Dennis said. "I think I found what might have been his hat. I think he was a cowboy or a mountain man." Ben was watching Ed and said "Once an archeologist always an archeologist."

Ed said "You got that right. I miss it but you can't make a living at it. Alright let's roll all this up. We still need to keep this just between us. I'll take it home with me and see what clues I can find." Ben said "First let me take some pictures." Ed said "I knew there was a good reason I brought you along" and smiled at Ben. "Good thinking."

"After you finish would you men like to stay for dinner?" I asked.

Ed said "I don't think so, it's getting pretty late. What do you think Ben?" Ben said, "Yeah, I guess as soon as I finish taking pictures we need to head home. My wife will be looking for me. "Ok let's get it done," Ed said.

They finished about a half hour later with the pictures and were getting ready to leave. After, they got washed up. Ed said "I sure enjoyed that delicious lunch, and for the great time we had here, it's been a long time since I did a dig. Ben said "Oh yes indeed, I get such a big kick out of watching Ed get so excited. I said "You got pretty excited yourself Ben! He just grinned.

I told them maybe they would like to bring their wives for a visit sometime. They both agreed. We'll keep in touch for sure. They put the Lone Stranger in the truck of Ed's car and waved goodbye.

Dennis was going to go back into the chicken coop, to do some more digging, but I told him to go wash up and have some dinner first. I told the kids the same thing. They all went out to the pump to wash up; I went in to make dinner.

There was quite a discussion at dinner. The kids wanted to help dad. I think they were hoping they would be the one to find something. Of course, the boys wanted to know if they could put their hideout back. Dad said "It might be awhile before we can put it back, but when we do, I will help you and it will be really a good one."

We did have some interesting conversations at dinner time. I was still concerned how the kids felt about finding bones that they dug up. Jill said "Their just bones mom." The rest of the kids agreed. "Well, ok." I said. I wasn't going to push that any further. After dinner was finished, Dennis said "Come on kids lets go. We are burning daylight.

Chapter 19

THE KIDS JUMPED UP AND headed out to the dig, within a minute I was sitting at the table by myself. "Oh well" I said with a sigh. As I sat there I thought it was like when we let the young cattle out of the barn in the mornings. The way the kids went rushing out the door. It made me laugh. Darren poked his head back in the door and said "Come on Carl."

My family didn't come back into the cabin till it started to get dark. By the look on their faces they hadn't found anything. I asked, well did you find anything? "Not yet, Carl just sat down in the dirt, he didn't seem interested at all." Dennis said with a laugh.

Dennis said "I think Lone Stranger, must have been robbed, there doesn't seem to be anything that a man would need to survive. I thought sure we would find a coffee pot or a canteen or maybe a frying pan, in that area. I guess we will have to wait and see what Ed finds out.

"I wonder if he had a horse." Chris asked. I guess we'll never know, I told him.

"May be a bear killed him." Denny said. No, I don't think so, his bones would be scattered all over, instead of in one place, I told Denny.

"Maybe he was shot." Jolynn said. Well if he was shot it wasn't in the head, because there was no hole in his skull, I told her.

"Well maybe he had a heart attack." Jill said. It could very well be. Well Sharlene what do you think? "I think he died of loneliness." Sharlene said.

You know that might very well be true. Whatever happened to him, he's in heaven now, I told all of the kids.

I woke up early knowing it was Sunday! We can get the chores done and breakfast over with. I was looking forward to going to church. The kids really liked Sunday school. I enjoy church; we have so much to be thankful for.

I started to get up out of bed and Dennis woke up and grabbed a hold of me and tried to pull me back in bed. He said "Just a little while longer honey." No we got a lot to do before we go to church, I said.

"Ok, do you want me to start the fire?" He asked. Yes, we will need hot water to wash and you need to shave I told him. I called the kids to get up; we're having cereal for breakfast.

After we got everything done we headed out for church. I mentioned to Dennis that after church he could talk to old Mr. Johnson. He might be able to tell us something about the history of Dixie Mountain. Dennis said, "Sounds like a plan, he loves to talk!"

The preacher gave a very positive sermon, about how God loves us and to be good to one another, not a word about if we were bad we would go to "hell."

After church Dennis was busy talking to Mr. Johnson. I met this woman, named Agatha, who was visiting some relatives in the area. All she could talk about was the trip she was going to take with her husband Frank. They were going on a trip around the islands in the Atlantic Ocean. So I didn't even try to get any information about Dixie Mountain, because I couldn't get a word in at all. She wasn't from this area anyway.

On the way home the kids were talking about Sunday school. They liked the way the teacher did a picture story about Jesus. When we got home I started fixing lunch while the kids went out to play.

Dennis sat down at the table waiting for a cup of coffee. He said "Well do you want to know what I found out?" I said; yes tell me, I told him I was disappointed that I was unable to find out anything myself. Dennis had been talking to Mr. and Mrs. Johnson for a long time after church.

Dennis got up and poured himself a cup of coffee and sat back down at the table. Let's wait till after lunch, I want the kids to hear this. When we were all settled down after lunch, we were ready to hear the story, the kids were all ears.

Chapter 20

DENNIS WAS READY TO TELL his story, as we all sat around waiting for him to start. He told us he had talked to Mr. Johnson and he told him, that Mrs. Johnson and him came west in a wagon train. The Johnson's settled in Clatskanie before it was a town. Dennis asked him, "Were there many others that settled here with you or passed away on the trail?" Mr. Johnson said they only had one death on the way out here. It was a childless couple, they kept to themselves. They seemed very secretive like they were running away from something.

The lady became very ill, and passed away about half way here. Never knew their names, I think they joined the wagon train a few miles out of Kansas.

Mrs. Johnson who was in a wheel chair was listening to them, she interrupted and said "I remember them; the woman was buried out on the prairie." Mr. Johnson said, "That he remembers seeing a stranger in town, and he had sold everything that he bought with them. He tried to talk to him but he just gave him a stern look and walked away, I never saw him again.

Now the image is focused.

Mrs. Johnson told Dennis, he was very tall, well built, and a short beard. She remembered him because he was so strong. He was always helping out with the heavy work. Mr. Johnson told me at that time there were some mountain men that came into town, but he never saw the stranger again nor could he remember his name.

Mrs. Johnson wanted to get home so Dennis shook their hands and thanked them for the interesting talk. As they went away Mr. Johnson said "Next time I will tell you about the adventures on the trail."

That's quite a story; I thought you were talking a long time. I'm glad the church has a play yard out back. The Johnson didn't wonder why you were so curious. "No I guess old folks just like to talk." Dennis said. Did you notice how they kept calling him the stranger? I asked. "Yes, I did." Dennis answered.

Ok, kids it time to get to work, they all started to complain and Dennis gave the kids the "Look" and they all ran up stairs to change their clothes.

"By the way did you know that Ed's wife works at the court house and Ben's wife works at the library?" Dennis asked me. I said, no I didn't know, do you think the guys will get the wife's to help out? "You can bet on it!" He said.

"Tell me honey what would you like if we get all that money?" He asked. Most of all I want to make sure the kids get to go to college. It would be nice to have a big house with lots of room for the kids, I said.

"Well that goes without saying. What would you want for yourself? He asked. I think I would like some time to do some painting or a little writing, I said.

"You mean you don't want some pretty clothes?" Dennis asked.

That's not important to me. I don't have much time to socialize when you have a family to raise. I asked him, what do you want?

He hesitated; looking thoughtful he said "I would like to have a ranch where we could raise cattle and horses."

We already have a good start on that! We already have cattle, why do you want horses?

"Yeah, but it's not big enough, you need to have enough land to also raise a hay crop. We'll need the horses to catch the cattle. If we get a big enough place we could, just ride them for fun," Dennis said.

How big are you talking about? I asked him. Oh a hundred acres or so, I don't want it real big. The kids would love it, he said. Well Dennis we can't really make any plans until we know everything is on the up and up, I reminded him.

Dennis said as he got up to leave, "I know, I guess I'll finish up filling the holes we dug in the chicken coop and put the boy's hide out back up."

I followed him out, to watch the fun. I heard him call the kids to come help. Just as I went out the door I heard a car coming down the road. I stopped to see who it was. It was my sister Simone and her two boys, who were close in age to our boys. They jumped out of the car and started to run to find the kids. I grabbed them and said "Hey don't I get a hug?" They gave me a quick hug and said "Hi Aunt Lola, where are the kids?" I told them they were in the chicken coop making a hide out. "Cool see ya," and away they went to join them.

Simone got out of the car and said "Whew, what a long drive." I went over to the car and said "Hi sis." We gave each other a hug. Then I asked her where her husband Bob was. She told me he was out fishing with the guy's so she thought the boy's and her would come see what we were up too.

"I brought you something." she said. She reached into the car and brought out a very large hat, almost as big as a sombrero, decorated with flowers. She was smiling mischievously. That is one ugly hat, I told her. I gave her the "Look." She said "It's to wear in the garden," I said, what garden, you know I don't have time for a garden. We both started to laugh, as I put the hat on her head. She gave a silly little dance, we laughed some more. We always have a good time together.

I said, come on let's see what's going on in the chicken coop. Just as we came in the door we heard Chris say "Do we get a floor?" "You will have a regular hide out floor. Everybody get over here and start stomping the dirt down. Make it really hard." Dad said. He looked up and said "Hi Simone! Would you like to join in?" She replied "No thanks, I left my stomping shoes at home."

When you get seven kids stomping, the dirt gets hard pretty fast.

Darren and Richard [Simone youngest boy] were in the far corner playing with toy cars. Her other two boys were really stomping. They were having a great time; our three girls were really going at it too.

Denny said "Hey mom, daddy said we get a door and a window." Great, I said.

While the kids were stomping, Dennis took a break and came over and gave Simone a hug. He said "How are you doing honey? Where is Bob?" Simone said "Oh, you know he's out fishing with the guys."

Just then Dennis turned and said "Wait a minute you kids!" He went back to the project. Simone and I looked at each other; he didn't seem to notice the crazy hat. Simone whispered to me, "He didn't even notice the hat." I said he would have if I was wearing it. Simone put the hat on my head. Then we went to the cabin to visit. I was dying to tell her about the treasure, but I can't yet. I'm sure going to hear from her when she does find out.

The time pasted so fast while she was there visiting. I asked her to stay for something to eat, but she said she had promised the boys that she would take them to McDonalds. They stayed as long as they could, but they had to get home. It was a great Sunday.

That evening after Dennis and I went to bed, we started talking about the day. I asked him if he got the dirt stomped down. He answered "Yeah, and then the kids all went out to take a look at the outhouse. They got a big kick out of it when Jolynn told them about the chicken falling down the hole and how the chicken climbed up the ladder. Then they had to check out the pond and the hand water pump. All in all I think they had a good time, Simone's boys didn't want to leave.

Did you start the hideout yet? I asked.

"No not yet, I have to find some lumber. I've got a good plan though. Maybe a window they can open with a rope and a back door to escape in case of an Indian attack." I laughed and said you are really getting in to it, aren't you? Dennis replied "It makes me feel like a kid again, he had a boyish smile on his face.

I told Dennis, that I'll see if I can find some lumber around the barn. I know there is some up in the barn. Maybe there is some in the back end of the cabin, that goes back up against the hillside.

"You be careful back there the floor is pretty rotten." He warned me.

We both drifted off to sleep.

Chapter 21

IN THE MORNING DENNIS WENT off to work after building the fire and having a quick breakfast. The kids were sleeping in, I decided to let them sleep and I would go out and get the chores done. We were getting more eggs from the chickens now. The cattle are pretty much on their own. I need to get some water on to heat for the kids, so they can wash up with, when they get up.

When I came back in from doing chores the kids were up getting their cereal for breakfast. What great kids, I gave them some peaches to go with their cereal and joined them for breakfast.

I needed to go to the back part of the cabin, to see if I could find the wood and clean it out, if possible. I was in no hurry; it was really spooky out there. Who knows what's back there, so far I had no trouble avoiding going back to that part of the cabin.

It looked like a long time ago someone tried to make an extension on to the cabin. The boards on the outside wall were coming loose and some had fallen part way down, letting daylight come into room.

There was no foundation; I didn't know what was under the floor. The whole thing went about eight yards back to the hillside.

There were holes in the sagging roof. I thought we got to do something about this, like tear it down! I stood there looking at the mess. I was glad we told the kids to stay out of here because it didn't look safe. They probably thought it was too scary to go into anyway.

I was still standing there and got a little shiver, thinking there's probably all kinds of things back there, like spiders and mice nest, I didn't even want to think about rats.

Maybe I should wait for Dennis to get home. No, I thought he has too much to do already. Maybe I could at least clear a path, if I can get the kids settled down doing something.

Let's see I need gloves, hat, a broom, bug spray and I will also need some tools. I told myself I can do this! As I got started the kids wanted to know what I was doing. You kids stay back; I'm going to make a path so we can clean up this mess, I told them. They wanted to help. I thought about it, and decide why not. Ok, Chris and Denny you can take the old boards outside when I give them to you. Sharlene you can take the bug spray and spray any bugs you see. Jill you take the broom and get the spider webs down. Jolynn you can get the tools and hand them to me and help the boys. First I'll make all of you a hat; it's so dirty back here. Come on back into the cabin, so I can fix you a granny hat. I took six pieces of cloth and tied a knot in each corner, to make them fit the head of each one of them, it worked out great. Ok, kids let's do this.

Once I got a safe place for us to walk, I started to take out the windows. I had Jolynn hand me the crow bar and hammer. It didn't take much, the frames were pretty rotten. I told the kids they could throw all the stuff we were going to burn out the window. I imagine they thought oh, good, another bon fire.

About an hour and a half things were going good. We had a pile of glass bottles, broken dishes, and tin cans. There's a pile for burning later and a pile of good boards that we could use. The kids were doing a great job!

Sharlene had really found a lot of bugs to spray. I had to calm her down; it was getting hard to breathe. Jill was running out of spider webs to sweep down. Jolynn, Chris and Denny were really getting a good size burn pile. They said "The bigger the better." They remembered the last one we had.

Darren had found a plate with a painting of a rather old looking couple holding pitch forks, with a farm scene behind them. I straighten up and looked over at Darren; he had also found a dirty old leather vest, and was going to try it on. "No, no, Darren." I said. I took it away from him and shook it out. It didn't look to bad and it didn't look that old. Of course, it was too large for him but he wanted to try it on. I thought what the heck. So I put it on him, it came down below his knees. He didn't want to take it off; I let him wear it for awhile.

I was glad I had the fore thought to make the granny hats. We must have looked quite a sight. Jill was really covered with dust, from all the sweeping. I knew it was going to be a bath night. I was amazed; they were so young to be doing all of this. They were so caught up in the work. I guess with no T.V. they were either bored or it was an adventure to them.

As we got closer to the hillside we found this glass box, it looked like it could have been a terrarium. It was covered with vines and weeds growing inside. There was a lot of dirt in the bottom. The glass was covered with a green scum. It was about 2ft. high and 2ft. wide and 4ft. long. Sure made me wonder what was going on here all these past years.

There was no wall against the hillside, just weeds and withered berry vines. It looked like there was something behind it! We were so excited. I couldn't stand it. I had to see what was behind there. "Ok, tool girl [Jolynn] see if you can find some cutters." I said. She ran off in a hurry, she knew where they were. While we waited, I looked around at what we had done so far. I couldn't believe how these little kids and one woman could accomplish so much. I was a proud momma!

Jolynn returned with the cutters. I found some gloves for Jill and Sharlene, so they could drag the vines out to the burn pile. The vines still had stickers on them. They started to take them out to the burn pile; the other kids gathered the weeds to burn. We were just getting started when Dennis showed up he said "Hey what's going on? He walked into the back of the cabin and saw what we had done and said "What a good job, there is quite a mess outside."

The kids were so excited, they all started to talk at once! He walked over to me; I had a big smile on my face."

Come look what we found." I said. He came closer, "It looks like a cave!!" He said. The kids were all still all talking at once. Ok! Ok! Calm down he told them. He reached over and took the cutters from me to make the opening larger. I was so glad he was there. He got the hole large enough for all of us to see in. We were all crowded around trying to see into the dark cave. Dennis asked "Which one of you knows where the flashlight is?" Denny piped up "I know I'll get it."

While we were all waiting, Dennis and I looked at each other with a big smile. Dennis said "I think we really found something, I can't wait to tell Ed and Ben." Denny came back with our big flashlight and gave it to his dad. Dennis told the kids "All right kids here we go. Better wait till I check it out, then you can come in." We waited and then we heard him say "It's pretty big. Come on in, I can stand up. Be careful." We went in very carefully and waited for our eyes to adjust to the darkness.

The cave was not very wide and the floor was littered with rock rubble. We couldn't see very well at all. Dennis was looking around with the flashlight. He said "I can't tell how safe it is in here. We better leave, I'll see if Ed can get some flood lights.

Denny said "Can we have this for our hide out?" Chris joined in "It would be so cool." Jolynn said "Ok, us girls get your other hide out." Then Jill said "It's not much of a hide out if everyone knows where it is." Sharlene had to put her two cents in "It could be a play house for us girls." Darren had to have his say "I want a hide out too."

Dennis said "No one gets anything till Ed checks it out." While he was talking he was checking out the cave with the flash light.

As we were all leaving the cave, I looked at my watch, and said "My goodness we have been at this all day. I know you kids must be hungry and tired. Momma will have dinner ready in a little while, we can work on this tomorrow, now get washed up.

Dennis looked around at his little troop, and said "Those are quite the caps you made the kids, you all looked pretty funny!" I replied "The look on your face, when you saw the cave was pretty hilarious." He just said "I'm hungry." It was a long evening, getting dinner and getting all the kids washed up. We were all pretty dirty.

Finally Dennis and I had a chance to talk. He told me he was going to talk to Ed after work and see when he wanted to check out the cave. We started talking about the Lone Stranger. There are so many scenarios about the man. Maybe he was a mountain man, or maybe he was a thief hiding out. Maybe, Greta and he were running away from family. Maybe they just wanted to come west for the adventure. I think he must have had some education, from what I could tell from his letter. He must have been very old or sick when he wrote it.

"I think we need to wait and see what Ed comes up with, after he gets a chance to check out the cave." Dennis said. I said "I would like to know more about the Lone Stranger. We made our way up the stairs to bed." Just before we fell asleep I told Dennis I was going into town to get groceries, in the morning.

Getting groceries was no easy task. When we arrived at the store I told the kids to stay close to me. They were good about it, but I always ended up with extra things I did not put in the basket. They had been working so hard with me I pretended not to notice.

When we got back home, I fed the kids and we got the chores caught up. I thought we could get some more cleaning done in the back part of the cabin. I was anxious to see what was in the boxes. First I have to load up the rotten boards and the trash we were going to burn. But we'll have to wait until tomorrow to get started.

Chapter 22

I TOLD DENNIS I HAVE a busy day tomorrow. I have to do some shopping for a present for Lila's birthday present."

Who? He said

Lila, Lily daughter!

I thought to myself, what can you buy a little girl who likes to drown a kitten. I found a nice sweater for her; at least she can't break it. After the birthday party, I was hoping to do some more work on the back of the house, to finish cleaning it out.

But we still need to go to Lila birthday party today, I had the present wrapped and ready to go. The kids really didn't want to go! "She's mean mom." Jill said.

We don't have to stay long. Maybe you will have cake and ice cream. We got into the car and drove to their house. I knocked on the door and Lila answered. I said, Hello Lila we are here for your birthday party. She gave me a mean look and walked away. Lily came to the door and said "Please come in she's just a little upset today." We went in, I told Lila we had a present for her and held it out to her. She grabbed it and tore it open and said "I don't want a dumb sweater and threw it on the floor." Then she stomped off to her room. Lily was so embarrassed, "I'm so sorry I just can't handle it any more. She's leaving to go where she can get counseling."

I suggested that we should go, I am so sorry, and that it turn out this way. I didn't know what to do to help. It caught me off guard. As we left I was listening to the kids, they were saying; that was mean of her, we didn't get any cake, I don't care, we should have kept the present. I told them some people have problems, maybe she will get some help. Tell you what when we get home I'll make some peanut butter cookies. How's that? I said. One of them yelled, Yeah! I don't think Darren quite understood what was going on but he liked peanut butter cookies!

Chapter 23

AFTER THE BIRTHDAY PARTY DISASTER I decide it would be a good time to do more clean up. I went out and backed up the pickup to where I could load it up. I asked the kids if they wanted to help. They all agreed but they were not too happy about it. They wanted to know when we were going to have the bon fire. I told them when we get all the trash cleaned up. It took some time to load up what we had thrown out the window. But there was at least one more load to do.

Finally, we got to go through the rest of the trash. There were only three cardboard boxes. The first box was encouraging; there was an old crank telephone on top of some old newspapers and magazines. I thought maybe there might be some clues from the dates. We put them in one corner for Ed to look over. The crank telephone look good, I wanted to keep it. I had Chris put it in the house, by this time we decided to call it a day.

Later that evening Dennis told me he had talked to Ed after he got off work. He told him about finding the cave. Ed and Ben wanted to come out the next day and they would bring out a flood light to be able to see into the cave.

The next morning about ten o'clock, we heard a car pull up to the house. The kids and I went out to see who it was. I figured it would be Ed and Ben. Sure enough it was. They were smiling when we greeted each other. I shook hands with them. All of the kids had to shake hands too. Ed and Ben started to get some equipment out of the trunk of the car. They handed some tools for the kids to carry, Ben carried the big flood lights. As they were carrying everything into the back end of the house, they were talking. Ed said "We have a lot to tell you and Dennis. Ben spoke up and said "We would like to wait for Dennis to get home, just so we can talk to the both of you at the same time, if you don't mind. I told them it was fine with me as I tagged along behind them. Ben handed me the extension cord for the light. I hurried off to plug it in. They both were in a hurry to get started. I didn't even get a chance to offer them coffee. When I came back they were in the cave setting up the flood lights.

The kids and I were standing outside of the cave, waiting to hand them the tools. We could hear them talking excitedly to each other. Ben came out of the cave and took the tools from the kids. He looked at me and told me they were going to check out the back part of the cave. Ed thought the cave might have been larger at one time but caved in.

I told Ben that I would check on them to see if they needed anything. "Ok" he said as he disappeared back into the cave. I took a pitcher of water and two cups and set them outside of the cave. They were in the cave for an almost two hours. I couldn't help myself; I had to go see how they were doing. There was a pile of dirt that they had dug out from the back end of the cave.

It was about time for Dennis to come home. I thought I had better see what I could fix for dinner. Ben and Ed must be getting hungry. Dennis arrived shortly; he came into the cabin and said "I see the guys are here, they are in the cave right?" I told him "Yes, they have been here awhile." I barely got the words out of my mouth and he was headed back toward the cave. I've never seen guys so excited. Five minutes later he was back and wanted to know where the wheel barrow was. I told him and he was gone again.

The next thing I knew they had knocked out the boards on the outside wall, next to the cave. Dennis was hauling dirt out of the cave.

I had dinner ready. I fed the kids and went out to the cave. The men were real dirty and look exhausted, I hollered at them. "Stop right now, all of you are exhausted. Go get washed up and have some dinner! Now! They all stopped and looked at me. Ben exclaimed "A sassy little gal isn't she, but she is right. I'm so hungry, I feel like I'm going to faint, as he grinned. I almost laughed, Ed's hair was a mess and full of dirt. Ben's bald head had dirt and sweat on it. All of them were covered with dust. I could tell Dennis was tired after a day at work and now he was hauling dirt.

I said "You need to think this through." I didn't know how they would respond. To my surprise they agreed. Ed and Ben were not used to this kind of hard work, they needed to slow down.

Chapter 24

AFTER DINNER BEN WANTED TO tell Dennis and me the good news about the treasure. According to all the research my wife Clara, has done about the money, coins, and jewelry is yours! Ben told us "I would like to set up an account at your bank, so we can deposit funds we receive for the treasure. I need you to meet Ed and me at the bank to set it up. Also I will give you an accounting with each transaction. Ed has drawn up all the legal papers for us. Ok. Ed it's your turn.

Ed then told us he had a friend named Terry that had worked with him on a lot of excavations. He would help with the work and not expect any pay. He would do it for the experience and the excitement. Ed told us that if we find more items in the back of the cave, it could be a game changer.

Dennis told them, we have known you for many years, and I think it's safe to leave it in your hands; whatever you decide is right for us. Ed said "It's nice of you to say so. Well I think we've did enough for today, I hate to leave. We'll have to figure out the time when we can get some full days in.

As they were leaving Ed told Dennis they would try to make it out the coming week end, if not sooner. We had arranged earlier to meet Ben and Ed in town at the bank. A special account was set up, papers were signed. So now we had a trust fund and money in the bank. Ben all ready has some buyers for the silver certificates. He's a busy little guy!

When we got home that day, I had to take the sitter home. When I got back from dropping the sitter off, Dennis was home and hauling dirt out of the cave, he was almost finished moving all the dirt that they had dug out of the cave so far.

The kids were busy throwing some more trash into the pickup. They seemed to be enjoying themselves. When they saw me, little Darren yelled "Mommy's home." All of them came over and gave me a hug. I was only gone a half hour, but it sure felt good. Now I know how Dennis feels when the kids greet him when he comes home.

After dinner we went back to work, the kids and I had got all the trash loaded into the pickup. All of junk that was left, we still had to go through again, you never know what we may of missed and we might want to keep some of it. We ended up keeping the old telephone, the old newspapers for Ed, a picture of an Indian chief and a small statue of a dog. Dennis asked me "Where is that small broken table you found?" Its over by the chicken coop, I thought you might want to fix it for the boy's hide out." I answered.

I heard Chris say "Hey Denny, dads going to fix the table for our hide out." I looked over at Denny, who was holding the picture of the Indian chief. He said "Can we have this picture of the Indian to hang up?" I answered "Sure for now." Dad turned too little Darren and asked him "By the way Darren where is that leather vest you found?" Darren's eyes lit up and he said "I'll get it daddy." It took him about two minutes. When he came back he was wearing the vest. He had a big smile on his face. Dad took a look at him and said "Oh! That is nice, it's really too big on you son. I'll tell you what, suppose you let daddy wear it till you get bigger. I will not let anyone have it. It is yours but daddy will take care of it. What do you think?" He looked at his dad and said "Ok, but it is still mine." He took it off and gave it to his dad. Dennis tried it on and it fit perfectly. "Ok, boys let's get your hideout fixed up." Dad said.

"How about us girls?" Jolynn wanted to know. I quickly said, you girls are going to help me plan where to have the bon fire. We won't be having it for a while but we want to be ready. So we all were kept busy the rest of the afternoon.

Chapter 25

IT WAS A WARM SUNNY morning; it was Saturday July 10th. Ed showed up with a car load of people. It turned out that Ed and Ben brought their wives with them. Also Terry, the friend Ed had mentioned to us. The wives didn't wait to be introduced. "Hi, I'm Rose, Ed's wife." "Hi, I'm Clara, Ben's wife. Rose spoke up and said "We are so excited to be here, the boys have gotten us so involved in this whole thing."

I took an instant like to both of the women. Terry reached over and shook hands with Dennis and me. About that time the kids came over to say hello. Terry spoke up and said "What a lovely family." I replied "Well thank you Terry." Terry was a very large man, more muscle than fat, dark hair and very brown eyes. My guess would be he was around fifty years old; he had a very warm personality.

The gals, I would guess are somewhere in their thirty's. Clara is a natural blond with pretty blue eyes and a great smile. She is very slim and professional looking. Rose had dark hair and very beautiful, with bright green eyes. She was well endowed; she was one of the down to earth types. They both were around five feet six.

I knew we all were going to be good friends. Although, I felt a little shabby, I was wearing jeans and an old sweat shirt.

Ed said "I have something to show Dennis and Lola. Let's go into the house." Then he turned to Ben and said "How about you show Terry the cave. By the way Terry and the girls know about everything. Clara and Rose you come with us. Both of you will get a chance to look around when we get done talking." No one said a word, just went where Ed told them to go. I guess he was the organizing boss.

The kids went with Ben and Terry out to the cave. As Ed, Clara, Rose, Dennis and I settled around the table. Ed began talking, "As you know the Lone Stranger's bones went to forensic lab. From what they could tell he died of some natural causes. They reproduced his facial features from the skull. When the bones were cleaned they found some whisker hair, so he had a beard. Also, some hair they found was dark, which had to come from his scalp. I have a picture; he took it out of his pocket and laid it on the table." Clara and Rose were smiling as Dennis and I looked at the picture, I was amazed, as was Dennis. The picture showed him as quite good looking. His not at all like I pictured him in my mind. I said "Wow"

Lone Stranger

Dennis said Amazing."

Clara spoke up "I've been going through a lot of records at the court house. I found in the immigration records that he and

Greta came from England, the time line fit. They were married and both were white. You don't have to call him the Lone Stranger any longer. His name is Sir Edward Samuel Baker. They were both explorers, they didn't come out west with the wagon train.

Rose spoke up next "I found nothing at the library, in any of the newspaper articles that I looked at. There was no record of any fortune lost or stolen during this time. What I mean to say, no criminal records were found. They must have acquired the fortune as an investment after they were in the states before 1928. So if they had that kind of money, they must have come west on the train. Of course, there is no record of that. All we can think is they were exploring this part of the country.

Now Ed said "We don't know what happened to Greta. I suspect we just might find her in the cave. I guess we will have to wait and see. Ladies, do you have any more to say? Clara and Rose shook their heads no. "Alright then, Dennis lets go join the guys in the cave." Ed said.

I noticed Rose and Clara had tennis shoes on instead of high heels. I asked them if they would like to go look around. I told them we could go see the cave first, then show them where we found the treasure and the Lone Stanger. "Don't you mean Sir Edward Baker?" Rose asked with a smile. I looked at her and answered, "Oh, yeah that's right."

As we headed back toward the cave, Clara said "Ed told me your dog Carl is responsible for finding the treasure. Do you think he might be possessed? I answered, I don't know for sure but he acts mighty strange at times. Clara didn't want to give up on the subject. She said "I've never heard of a dog being possessed. Have you Rose?" Rose just shagged her shoulders. Clara continued "Rose won't admit it, but she sometimes has physic powers." Clara said "Sorry Rose." That ended the subject.

As we neared the cave we saw the guy's busy digging and hauling the dirt. All the kids were waiting anxiously to see what they might find.

Carl {the dog} spotted Rose and came up to her and jumped at her then sat down and stared at her. Rose turned pale and had a blank look on her face. Clara took a hold of her and asked "Are you all right Rose?" Clara seemed very concerned. We were standing outside of the cave, Carl stayed right by her side. Rose was shaking; she reached down and picked up Carl. Clara and I stood there wondering what to do.

Ed came out of the cave; he had a look of concern on his face. He put his arm around her. He asked her "She's in there, isn't she?" She looked at him and shook her head, yes. He asked Rose, if she was alright, she nodded and put the dog down, he just sat there.

Rose took a deep breath and said "Her spirit is trapped in there. Sir Edward's spirit is trying to get to her, he won't leave without her. She cannot leave, I don't know why, I could hear her screaming. Oh please hurry Ed. Clara and I were standing there with tears in our eyes. Ed told us that it happens to her sometimes, but not this strong. Rose said "We must go into the cave, where is Carl?" I said, He's right here waiting for you, we went into the cave. The three of us and the kids stood back against the wall out of the way.

The guys went back to digging and hauling out the dirt. They were really going at it, Ben and Dennis were taking turns shoveling and hauling the dirt. Ed and Terry were digging around this large solid stone. They would have to try to pry it loose. Ed said "Stay back everyone we don't know what might happen." Terry got this very long crow bar, Dennis and Ben came over by us gals and the kids, Ed backed up.

Terry tried to pry the rock loose, it didn't move. Then he backed up and shrugged his shoulders, and then he grab the crow bar and pried with all his might. The rock started to come loose, he kept at it and it broke loose! Terry jumped out of the way. It rolled about two feet. There was an opening! A gust of cold air came rushing out. Then everything was so still. A strong warm feeling of love surrounded us.

Rose spoke softly and said "Sir Edward has found his Greta." We all stood there stunned. I swear we could see their spirits come together and there was something swirling around their feet. Just a few seconds and they were gone. The air returned to normal. Every one stood there not believing what they saw and felt.

Terry was standing there with his eyes bulging and his mouth open. He said "I have never! Never! Seen anything like that! Dennis looked like someone had turned him off. Ed just stood there with the most amazing look on his face. Clara and I were shaking so bad we couldn't say anything. The kids were looking at everyone, wondering what was going on. Rose had her hands clasped together looking upward. Our dog was lying stretched out on the ground, like he was unconscientious. Rose told us he was alright, Carl has left him.

Ed said "Ben can you get all this down while it's fresh in your mind?" Ben was still staring into space; he turned to Ed and said "My god! Ed gives me a minute." Dennis came around and said "The excitement around here never ends! We all started laughing.

When things settled down, Clara asked Rose what she had experienced, Rose told her to give her a minute.

Ed told everyone that the cave might not be safe inside the hole. He wanted everyone to leave the cave except Terry and him. He wanted to see if Greta's remains were in there. If so he wanted Terry to help him collect them.

The rest of us left the cave. We gathered around the picnic table out in the yard. Ben brought his writing tablet to the table and sat down. He wanted to hear what Rose had to say.

Rose felt ready to tell us what she experienced. She began "By the way the spirit in the cave was Greta's. Sir Edward and his wife Greta were on their way to Portland. Before they even got their camping gear unloaded they spotted the cave. Being explorers they didn't want to wait to take a look. They made a couple torches and went into the cave. They were only in the cave a few minutes; Carl (their dog) started snarling like he was in danger. It sounded like he was in a fight. Sir Edward told Greta to stay inside the cave. He took the torch and rushed out to help Carl! Carl was being attack by coyotes! Sir Edward chased them away but it was too late. Carl was badly hurt! He took him over to the front of the cave, and built a fire and tended his wounds.

Sir Edward hollered at Greta as loud as he could. She was in the very back part of the cave. Just then the earth started to shake it was an EARTH QUAKE! The earth shook so hard that the center of the cave collapsed.

When the earth quake hit, Sir Edward and the dog was spared. Except Sir Edward had fallen and hit his head on a rock and was knocked out cold. When he revived, the quake had stopped. He went into the cave and saw what had happened, he hollered as loud as he could for Greta, again and again! There was {No answer}.

He panic and started clawing at the rocks. It was no use; he was losing a lot of blood from the gash on his head, he passed out again. When he came too he was disoriented and it was night. He managed to get out of the cave; he saw the fire that he had built. It was about to go out, he put more wood on the fire. He noticed Carl laying there on the ground; he went over to him and realized he was hurt badly. Then it hit him what had happened. He started sobbing, my Greta! My Greta!

Rose paused for a moment, and then said "The vision just stopped, it was like a fast moving movie." We were all sitting there with tears running down our faces. I believe it was the first time I saw tears in my husband's eyes.

Rose continued "I have the feeling that Sir Edward must have lived on for some time. He never left the area. He must have buried the treasure to keep it from robbers. When his dog died he buried him on top of the treasure to miss lead anyone who might be digging around here. His spirit would not leave Greta behind. Greta's spirit felt trapped and couldn't pass on. I won't believe anything different." She looked exhausted.

Ed and Terry came out of the cave, carrying a box. I jumped up from the table and I said to Ed "I think you should take Rose into the house to rest, she looks pretty shook up. He looked at me and then at Rose. He turned to Terry and asked him to take the box and put it in the car. He went to Rose and said "I'm so sorry sweetheart; I got you into this whole thing." As they were walking toward the house I heard Rose say "I wouldn't have missed it for the world."

I looked around at the kids. They were all talking about what they saw. Little Darren said "I saw a doggy mama!" Jill said "We all did, didn't we?" Chris said "Can we see it again?" Denny said "Are they all going to heaven?" Jolynn answered "Of course they are." Sharlene said "I told you, he died of loneliness."

I thought I needed to distract them for a while. I said "Ok, kids we'll talk about this later. I think I promised we would have a bon fire, let's go!" I started to run toward the fire pile. The kids all jumped up from the table and ran after me. Dennis said "Ok, let's do this! Come on Ben, you too Terry. We get to start the fire! Ben replied "Yeah, we make fire! Clara jumped up and said "Wait for me!

Chapter 26

WHILE WE WERE WAITING FOR the fire to get started, our dog showed up, wagging his tail and barking. I looked at him and thought he is starting to act like a normal dog. I said to the kids "I think we need to change the dogs name back to Mutt. They all agreed, I think Mutt did too.

When Ed and Rose joined us, the fire was going good. Rose said she was feeling great. Terry took out his harmonica and started playing. Ben said "Good idea." He ran to the car and got his violin. Ben told us that he carried his violin with him almost everywhere. He turned to Terry and said "Let's give them a tune."

The kids started to dance around to the music. It was great! Us ladies got up and went to the house to get some food. Yes, wieners to roast too. When the fire started to die down and we had finished eating Clara declared, "We need to give Sir Edward and Greta a proper send off. We all agreed. Terry and Ben started playing softly "Amazing Grace." We all stood with our hands on our hearts, while Clara spoke. Heavenly father we commend the spirits of Sir Edward and Greta, also little Carl into your loving arms. Amen.

One more tune for the kids, then it was time for their bed time. They looked like they were all ready to go to bed; it had been a long day. After I got them all safely tucked into bed I returned to the fire.

Ed was ready to tell us about the remains they had found in the cave. He began "I'll tell you the facts first, as I have learned when I was an archaeologist. As we suspected the remains were female. She was about five foot three, white and had long hair. We found a wedding ring on her finger. Some of her clothing was not completely destroyed. We could tell she wore boots, long pants and a shirt and we found a hat. There was a torch that was not completely consumed. There couldn't have been much air left after the cave fell in. She must have died from suffocation. There is no way we can tell what color her eyes were.

We will know more after forensic studies the bones and the structure of her face. Then we know what she looked like. It shouldn't take long this time. I won't have to go through all the red tape. That's all for now, but I'll let you know if anything else turns up. It might be a good idea to board up the cave Dennis, it might not be safe." Dennis said "Sure no problem."

It was getting late, the fire was almost out. It was time to break up the party, although none of us really wanted to. We all said our good-byes and hope to see each other soon.

About a week later Ed and Terry showed up in the evening. Ed was anxious to show us the reconstruction of Greta's facial features. She was very pretty, I was so surprised how young she looked. Ed had also brought her wedding ring to show us and wanted to know what we wanted to do with it. It looked very expensive. Dennis and I looked at each other. I said we'll have to think it over. Ed said "No hurry."

Greta

Ed said "Terry and I would like to take one last look in the cave. Then we will pack up all the tools and the flood lights. First, I want to tell you something. When Rose was looking at the emigration records she found that Sir Edward and Greta came here from London, England. So their remains need to be shipped back to London to be buried there. We will need you to sign this document saying where they were found in case anything should come up later. You don't need to worry, I've got you covered." Dennis and I just sat there trying to absorb everything. I was so glad we could trust Ed. We signed the paper. "I guess they would like to be sent home.

Ed turned to Terry and said "Well let's get packing Terry." Terry turned to Dennis and remarked "Bossy, old boy isn't he," then winked at Dennis. "I haven't boarded up the cave yet." said Dennis. Terry said with a grin, "That's good to hear, because you know who would have to remove the boards." Dennis went out with them to see if he could help. I heard him say, "You guys, be careful, I would hate to have to dig you out, I heard them all laughing.

It didn't take the guys long to check out the cave and pack things up. I guess they didn't find anything else in the cave. I asked

Ed and Terry if they would like some coffee before they leave. Ed said "I think we should get going." I told them I had some peanut butter cookies. Terry replied "We have time Ed." Ed said as we headed toward the house "Oh! Yeah we love your peanut butter cookies."

We were all settled around the table, eating cookies and drinking coffee. Ed said "Well Dennis and Lola if you don't mind me asking, what plans do you for the future?" Dennis replied "We are selling our house in town and we have our eye on this small ranch not far from here." I spoke up and said "It has a four bedroom house on it and plumbing!" I had a big, big smile on my face. Dennis said "In fact we made an offer."

Terry spoke up and said "If you need any one to help with the moving, let me know. I would like to keep in touch with you, I love the country. Ed said with a grin "Can't you wait till you're invited Terry?" I answered for him. "All of you will always be welcome. We don't want to lose any of you. We consider you our friends, you always have been. Ed said "We feel the same." Dennis said "Oh you guys are getting mushy now." Ed said "I guess that's our clue to get going." We all laughed, Dennis and I walked them to the car to say so-long.

Dennis and I went back to the cabin and I went to check on the kids. They were all sleeping peacefully. We talked about everything that has happened that summer. As we were getting ready for bed, Dennis said "Well I guess that settles the Mystery of Dixie Mountain." I told him not quite, we still don't know about the lives of Sir Edward and Greta. There is a lot we don't know. He answered "As far as I am concerned it is."

I really didn't think the mystery was solved. The emigration people had them as explorers, but where were their maps and journals? What happened to all their supplies? Where and how did they acquire the fortune? So many questions, that is unanswered. I guess it will always be a Mystery! I'll have to leave it to your imagination!

THE END!